P9-DDY-720

#13.96 Renewed 10/20/04

WONDER WOMAN®

1 Am Wonder Woman

Written by Nina Jaffe

Illustrated by Ben Caldwell

Wonder Woman created by
William Moulton Marston

■ HarperFestival®
A Division of HarperCollins*Publishers*

Amazons live on Paradise Island.
Our home is far across the sea and
hidden under the clouds.

Amazons live in peace.

We hunt in the forest.

We spin tales, and dance to harps and drums

when the moon rises in the sky.

But my mother, the queen, was lonely.

One day, she shaped

a baby girl from

clay and wished

for a child.

The gods granted her wish and gave me life! I was named Diana, princess of the Amazons.

I was given special gifts
and wonderful powers.

I can fly like an eagle

and soar over the mountaintops.

I can speak with the animals—
even with the fish and the birds.

My eyes are
keen.
I can throw
my spear across the
valley—and always
hit my mark.

See my silver bracelets
flashing in the sunlight!
With their magic power,
I can ward off any weapon.

When I twirl my Golden
Lasso of Truth,
I can catch anyone who
tries to escape.

They have no choice.

They must tell me all their plans.

I can pick up a boulder

and balance it on the palm of my hand.

I can swim underwater and play tag with the dolphins.

Even though I can run the fastest and leap the highest, to laugh and play with my friends is best of all.

That is the Amazon way.

But when I look into our magic sphere,

I can see troubles in the world outside.

I see children who need food and clothing.

I see people fighting over land and water.

I see danger to the birds and the forests.

I know I have to do something to help.
I have been chosen to use my powers
for good.

And so, I say good-bye to Paradise Island.

Now, I've come to your world.

Sometimes I wear my tiara,
and carry my Amazon sword and shield.

Other times, I look just like everyone else.
You would never know my true identity.

But when someone needs help,

I will fly to the hot desert sands

or to the stormy sea.

Even stronger than my sword

and my Golden Lasso

is my message of justice and peace.

No one can stop me,

for I am Wonder Woman!